FUN FACT FILE: ENGINEERING MARVELS

20 FUN FACTS ABOUT FAMOUS SUBWAYS

BY JONATHAN AND MARIEL BARD

Gareth Stevens PUBLISHING

Please visit our website, www.garethstevens.com. For a free color catalog of all our high-quality books, call toll free 1-800-542-2595 or fax 1-877-542-2596.

Library of Congress Cataloging-in-Publication Data

Names: Bard, Jonathan. | Bard, Mariel.
Title: 20 fun facts about famous subways / Jonathan and Mariel Bard.
Description: New York : Gareth Stevens Publishing, 2020. | Series: Fun fact file: engineering marvels | Includes glossary and index.
Identifiers: ISBN 9781538246665 (pbk.) | ISBN 9781538246689 (library bound) | ISBN 9781538246672 (6 pack)
Subjects: LCSH: Subways–Juvenile literature.
Classifiction: LCC TF845.B37 2020 | DDC 625.4'2–dc23

First Edition

Published in 2020 by
Gareth Stevens Publishing
111 East 14th Street, Suite 349
New York, NY 10003

Designer: Sarah Liddell
Editor: Therese Shea

Photo credits: Cover, p. 1 (main) Baiterek Media/Shutterstock.com; file folder used throughout David Smart/Shutterstock.com; binder clip used throughout luckyraccoon/Shutterstock.com; wood grain background used throughout ARENA Creative/Shutterstock.com; p. 5 William Perugini/Shutterstock.com; p. 6 Bellomonte/Wikimedia Commons; p. 7 Kev Gregory/ Shutterstock.com; p. 8 Bleakcomb/Wikimedia Commons; p. 9 Guybrush Threepwood/ Wikimedia Commons; p. 10 LunaseeStudios/Shutterstock.com; pp. 11, 22 Felix Lipov/ Shutterstock.com; p. 12 Nick Photoworld/Shutterstock.com; p. 13 SVF2/Contributor/Universal Images Group/Getty Images; p. 14 Chie Inoue/Shutterstock.com; p. 15 littlenySTOCK/ Shutterstock.com; p. 16 Alexandre Rotenberg/Shutterstock.com; p. 17 UNIT 80/ Shutterstock.com; p. 18 BrockF5/Wikimedia Commons; p. 19 EvrenKalinbacak/ Shutterstock.com; p. 20 Michelle Baumbach/Shutterstock.com; p. 24 Andrew Stawicki/ Contributor/Toronto Star/Getty Images; p. 25 Jonathan Percy/Shutterstock.com; p. 26 YURI KADOBNOV/Staff/AFP/Getty Images; p. 27 Scdnr/Wikimedia Commons; p. 29 Charles Bowman/Shutterstock.com.

Printed in the United States of America

CPSIA compliance information: Batch #CW20GS: For further information contact Gareth Stevens, New York, New York at 1-800-542-2595.

CONTENTS

Words in the glossary appear in **bold** type the first time they are used in the text.

UNDERGROUND ENGINEERING

Most people on a subway don't give much thought to the **engineering** that makes it work. Instead, they're likely thinking about the next stop or whether they'll be on time to their destination, or the place they're traveling to.

In the time that subways have existed, **innovations** have taken them from smoky, uncomfortable ways to travel to driverless, smooth trains that are better for the **environment.** The millions of riders crowding into subways every day could tell you how important they are!

A subway is an underground railway system. With subway systems in over 175 cities around the world, it's easy to think of them as just a part of everyday life!

BEGINNINGS

FUN FACT: 1

SUBWAYS ARE OFTEN CALLED "METROS" BECAUSE OF A FRENCH COMPANY.

The business Compagnie du Chemin de Fer Métropolitain de Paris helped build and run the Paris subway system. People called the subway *le Métropolitain* and then *le Métro.*

The Paris *Métropolitain* first opened in 1900. In English, "metropolitan" means "having to do with a large city."

By 1869, trains powered by steam engines began running in the London Underground. By 1913, the subway became electric.

FUN FACT: 2

THE LONDON UNDERGROUND IS THE OLDEST SUBWAY SYSTEM IN THE WORLD.

The first tunnel, the Thames Tunnel, opened to visitors in 1843. In 1863, the first subway line opened to around 30,000 passengers, or riders. The next oldest subway—in Budapest, Hungary—didn't open until 1896.

The walls of London's subway tunnels were strengthened with iron so they don't cave in.

FUN FACT: 3

LONDONERS CALL THEIR SUBWAY "THE TUBE" BECAUSE OF SOME TUNNELS' ROUND SHAPE.

Many subway systems were built using the cut-and-cover method: Workers dug long pits and covered them to create tunnels. The London Underground started like this. Later, tools helped builders work completely underground to create tubelike tunnels without interrupting life aboveground.

WHAT A FIND!

FUN FACT: 4

CONSTRUCTION ON THE STATION CALLED SAN GIOVANNI IN ROME, ITALY, UNEARTHED OVER 40,000 ARTIFACTS!

The farther down the station passengers go, the farther back in time the artifacts are from.

Digging deep into the ground for this tunnel was a trip back in time. Artifacts included clay objects and even 2,000-year-old peach pits. Many are displayed in the subway station.

The La Brea Tar Pits are full of **fossils**, including those belonging to mammoths like the ones in this display. Mammoths were a kind of large, hairy elephant. They no longer exist.

FUN FACT: 5

MAMMOTH BONES INTERRUPTED CONSTRUCTION OF A SUBWAY LINE IN LOS ANGELES, CALIFORNIA!

After construction began in 2016, over 500 fossils were unearthed with the help of on-site scientists. The subway line goes by the La Brea Tar Pits, where many animals died over 11,000 years ago.

TRACES OF THE PAST

FUN FACT: 6

SOME SUBWAY STATIONS IN NEW YORK CITY WERE DESERTED.

The old City Hall station in New York City is still beautiful, even if it's not used anymore!

If you stay on the New York City Subway 6 train long enough, you can see a deserted station. A station near City Hall was finished in 1904, but closed in 1945 after another station was built that fit newer trains better.

The old wooden cars of the Subte were too expensive to fix, but two cars were put on display.

FUN FACT: 7

SOME WOODEN CARS OF THE BUENOS AIRES SUBWAY LASTED NEARLY 100 YEARS.

The Argentinian capital's subway system, called the Subte, opened in December 1913. It's the oldest metro in South America. The wooden cars on some lines were in use until 2013!

FUN FACT: 8

CERTAIN SUBWAY STATIONS HAVE BEEN USED AS BOMB SHELTERS!

Women and children camped in stations in Moscow, Russia, to survive attacks during World War II (1939–1945).

Stations in Russia, England, and Germany were marked with signs during wartime to let people know they could hide there. Deep underground is one of the safest spots to go in case of an attack.

CHANGE UNDERGROUND

FUN FACT: 9

SOME PEOPLE IN NEW YORK CITY USED THEIR MOUTHS TO SUCK SUBWAY TOKENS OUT OF MACHINES!

These people were hoping for a free ride. To fight this, workers sometimes sprayed machines with chili powder, giving thieves a spicy surprise! MetroCards took the place of tokens in 2003.

The Metropolitan Transportation Authority (MTA), which runs the subway, collected about 60 million tokens from passengers after MetroCards were put into use.

A man named Eric Bram first noticed the trend called the Pizza Principle in the 1960s, when both a slice of cheese pizza and a ride on the subway cost about 15 cents.

FUN FACT: 10

SINCE THE 1960s, A PIECE OF CHEESE PIZZA IN NEW YORK CITY HAS COST ABOUT THE SAME AS A SUBWAY RIDE.

The "Pizza Principle" is the idea that the prices of a piece of pizza and a subway ride have risen together. They remain nearly the same. This trend has been studied several times.

In Rio de Janeiro, Brazil, subway stations were decorated to look like Olympic events, such as tracks for running races!

FUN FACT: 11

HOSTING THE OLYMPICS USUALLY MEANS LOTS OF SUBWAY CONSTRUCTION FOR A CITY.

Before being flooded with visitors, cities often fix up subway lines or build new ones to support more people and new destinations. These preparations have helped improve **traffic** flow after the Olympics in some places.

FUN FACT: 12

ON ONE LINE OF THE PRAGUE SUBWAY IN THE CZECH REPUBLIC, EACH STATION HAS A DIFFERENT COLOR ON ITS WALLS.

The bubble-like **design** used for the walls in the Prague subway strengthens the metal!

On Line A in Prague, some colors stand for places. For example, gold is for the Prague Castle near the Hradčanská metro station and green is for the Royal Garden near the Malostranská station.

FUN FACT: 13

EVERY METRO STATION IN JAPAN HAS A SPECIAL SONG!

Instead of a loud buzzer, people hear a short tune that lets them know the train is about to leave. These songs have lessened people's **stress** and helped those who can't see well know where they are.

The writer of the Japanese subway station music, Minoru Mukaiya (pictured), says that if you put together all the tunes of a train line, it makes a whole song!

The station next to Arsenalna sits down in the valley, so putting Arsenalna around the same level avoids a steep hill for the trains to travel.

FUN FACT: 14

IT TAKES ABOUT 5 MINUTES TO RIDE THE ESCALATORS DOWN TO THE ARSENALNA METRO STATION IN KIEV, UKRAINE!

The entrance to the station sits at the top of a valley, and the station lies about 346 feet (105.5 m) below the ground. This station is deeper than the Statue of Liberty is tall!

IT'S GETTING CROWDED

FUN FACT: 15

THE SUBWAY IN TOKYO, JAPAN, CARRIES 8.7 MILLION PASSENGERS EACH DAY!

Nearly half of all people in Tokyo traveling to and from work use the rail system. Tokyo's metro is the busiest subway in the world. It carries more than 3 billion riders each year!

Tokyo's metro first opened in 1927.

WORLD'S BUSIEST SUBWAY SYSTEMS

RANK	LOCATION	NUMBER OF RIDERS PER YEAR
1	TOKYO, JAPAN	3,463,000,000
2	MOSCOW, RUSSIA	2,369,000,000
3	SHANGHAI, CHINA	2,044,000,000
4	BEIJING, CHINA	1,988,000,000
5	SEOUL, SOUTH KOREA	1,885,000,000
6	NEW YORK, NEW YORK	1,806,000,000
7	NEW DELHI, INDIA	1,789,000,000
8	GUANGZHOU, CHINA	1,730,000,000
9	MEXICO CITY, MEXICO	1,678,000,000
10	HONG KONG, CHINA	1,600,000,000

FUN FACT: 16

NEW YORK CITY'S SUBWAY HAS THE MOST SUBWAY STATIONS IN THE WORLD!

It has more than 470 stops serving 27 train lines. The world record for visiting every single station in the shortest amount of time is just under 21 1/2 hours!

Much of New York City's subway is underground, but the stop at Smith and 9th Streets is 88 feet (27 m) above the ground!

NEW YORK CITY SUBWAY SERVICES

1 BROADWAY / 7 AVENUE LOCAL
2 7 AVENUE EXPRESS
3 7 AVENUE EXPRESS

4 LEXINGTON AVENUE EXPRESS
5 LEXINGTON AVENUE EXPRESS
6 LEXINGTON AVENUE LOCAL

7 FLUSHING LOCAL

A 8 AVENUE EXPRESS
C 8 AVENUE LOCAL
E 8 AVENUE LOCAL

B 6 AVENUE EXPRESS
D 6 AVENUE EXPRESS
F 6 AVENUE LOCAL
M 6 AVENUE LOCAL

G BROOKLYN-QUEENS CROSSTOWN LOCAL

J NASSAU STREET LOCAL
Z NASSAU STREET EXPRESS

L 14 STREET-CANARSIE LOCAL

N BROADWAY EXPRESS
Q BROADWAY EXPRESS
R BROADWAY LOCAL
W BROADWAY LOCAL

S SHUTTLE SERVICES TO ROCKAWAY PARK, FRANKLIN AVENUE, 42 STREET

Local trains stop many times along a line. Express trains stop fewer times so that passengers can get places more quickly.

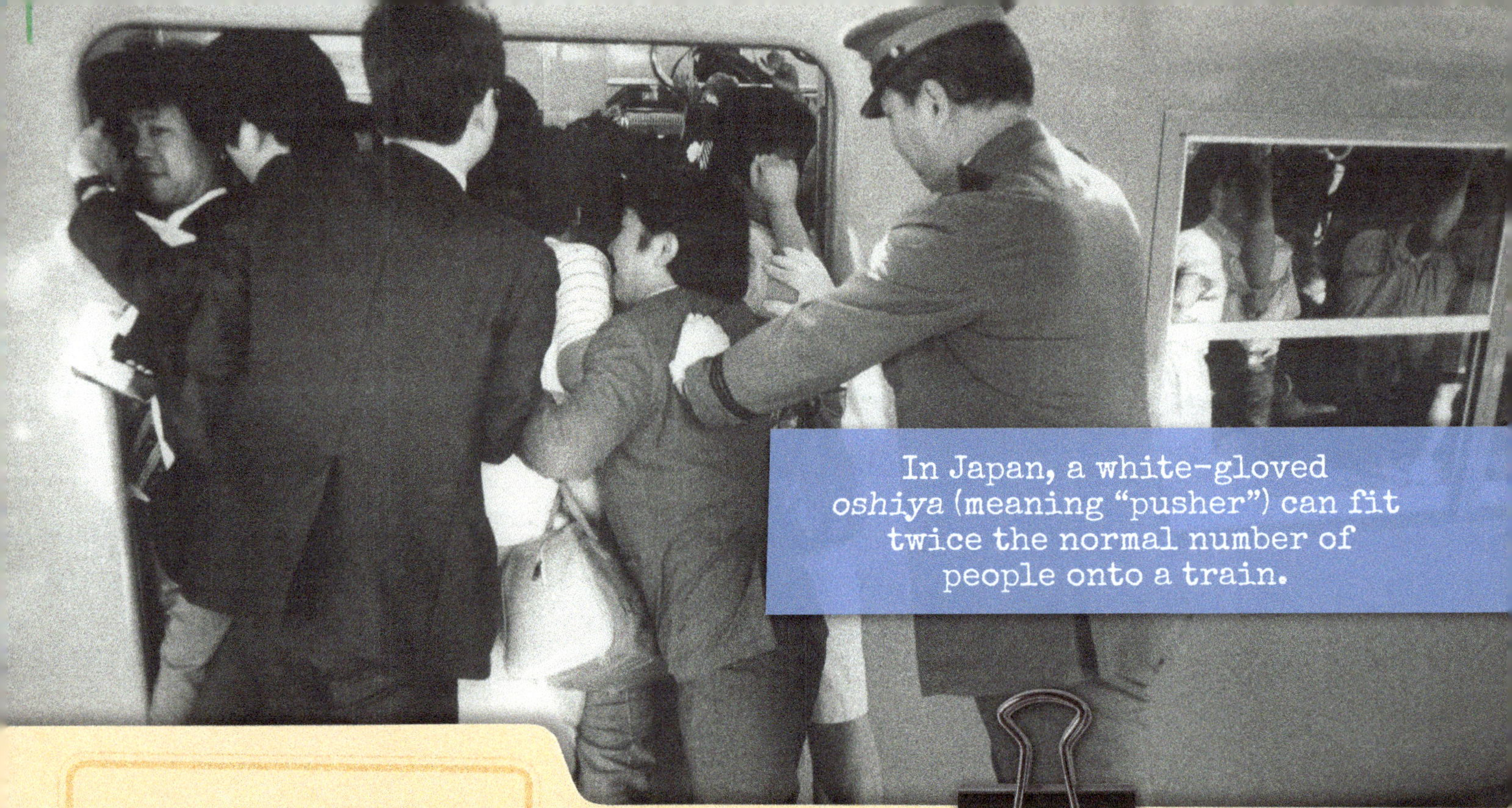

In Japan, a white-gloved *oshiya* (meaning "pusher") can fit twice the normal number of people onto a train.

FUN FACT: 17

IN SOME STATIONS, "PUSHERS" SHOVE PEOPLE INTO CROWDED SUBWAY CARS!

During the busiest hours, these workers make sure everyone gets on and no one gets caught in the doors. Subways in several countries, including China, Japan, and Spain, have used pushers.

INTO THE FUTURE

FUN FACT: 18

SOME METRO SYSTEMS DON'T HAVE DRIVERS!

Because there's no driver, passengers on this subway can sit at the front of the train and get a great view through a big window!

The driverless subway in Copenhagen, Denmark, is on time over 98 percent of the time. The driverless metro in Dubai in the United Arab Emirates is on time over 99 percent of the time!

FUN FACT: 19

SOME SUBWAY STATIONS HAVE UNUSUAL FARES FOR TRAIN TICKETS!

A Moscow station's squat-counting ticket machine was meant to get people excited about the 2014 Winter Olympics in Sochi, Russia. It also got them to exercise!

For a time, a subway ticket machine in a Moscow, Russia, subway station let passengers "pay" by doing exercises called squats. In Beijing, China, recycling plastic bottles helps people earn free metro trips!

Thousands of New York City subway cars have been sunk along the East Coast.

FUN FACT: 20

OLD SUBWAY CARS ARE BEING USED AS MAN-MADE REEFS!

After removing wheels, windows, doors, and any unsafe matter, subway cars were dropped in the Atlantic Ocean near Maryland in 2008. They became homes for all kinds of sea life.

TAKE THE TRAIN!

Next time you travel using a subway, take in all the innovations of engineering you see. Is your car cool in summer and warm in winter? Can you use **Wi-Fi** to check the internet? Maybe your train is traveling superfast and doesn't even have a driver! Subways will only get more user-friendly over time.

What may seem like a simple way to get from place to place is actually so much more than that. No matter where you're going, be sure to enjoy the ride!

A trip on the subway is an adventure! You have so many opportunities to learn new things about what's around you.

GLOSSARY

artifact: something made by humans in the past

bomb shelter: a place where people are guarded from dangerous blasts and weapons

design: the pattern or shape of something

engineering: the use of science and math to build better objects

environment: the natural world in which a plant or animal lives

escalator: moving stairs that carry people up or down

fossil: the marks or remains of plants and animals that formed over thousands or millions of years

innovation: a new way of doing things

reef: a chain of rocks or coral, or a ridge of sand, at or near the water's surface

stress: a state of concern, worry, or feeling nervous

token: a coin-like object that is used in place of money

traffic: the amount of people that move through a certain place

Wi-Fi: a way for electronic devices to wirelessly connect to the internet

FOR MORE INFORMATION

BOOKS

Hancock, James Gulliver. *How Cities Work: Explore the City Inside, Outside and Underground.* Oakland, CA: Lonely Planet Global Limited, 2016.

Hunt, Shannon, and James Gulliver Hancock. *Engineered! Engineering Design at Work.* Toronto, Ontario, Canada: Kids Can Press, 2017.

Rose, Simon. *Underground Transportation Systems.* New York, NY: Crabtree Publishing Company, 2019.

WEBSITES

Engineering Games
pbskids.org/games/engineering/
Try some fun-filled games all about engineering and problem-solving.

New York City Subway Facts for Kids
kids.kiddle.co/New_York_City_Subway
Read about the most complex subway in the world!

Publisher's note to educators and parents: Our editors have carefully reviewed these websites to ensure that they are suitable for students. Many websites change frequently, however, and we cannot guarantee that a site's future contents will continue to meet our high standards of quality and educational value. Be advised that students should be closely supervised whenever they access the internet.

INDEX